Josh and Dottie McDowell

KATIE'S
ADVENTURE AT
BLUEBERRY POND

Illustrated by Ann Neilsen

Chariot Books
David C. Cook Publishing Co.

To Kelly, Sean, Katie, and Heather
We love and adore each one of you.

Chariot Books is an imprint of David C. Cook Publishing Co.
David C. Cook Publishing Co., Elgin, Illinois 60120
David C. Cook Publishing Co., Weston, Ontario

KATIE'S ADVENTURE AT BLUEBERRY POND
© 1988 by Josh and Dottie McDowell for text and Ann Neilsen for
illustrations
Book design by Dawn Lauck

First Printing, 1988
Printed in the United States of America
93 92 91   5 4 3
LIBRARY OF CONGRESS
Library of Congress Cataloging-in-Publication Data
McDowell, Josh.
    Katie's adventure at Blueberry Pond/Josh and Dottie McDowell;
illustrated by Ann Neilsen.
        p. cm.
    Summary: Katie disobeys a family rule in going to the pond without
adult supervision, not realizing that grownups' rules are like God's rules
in that they represent love and protection. Includes discussion questions
at the end of the story.
    ISBN 1-55513-598-6
    [1. Ponds—Fiction. 2. Obedience—Fiction. 3. Christian life—
Fiction.] I. McDowell, Dottie. II. Neilsen, Ann, ill. III. Title.
    PZ7.M478446Kat 1988
[E]—dc19   88-14039
                                              CIP
                                              AC

DEAR PARENTS,

You and I have one of the most important responsibilities a person could ever have—caring for and raising a child. We know there are many temptations and pressures a child will face on his or her road to maturity. And we know rules are a big part of a child's life.

Katie's Adventure at Blueberry Pond, along with the discussion guide at the end of the story, will help you reinforce a powerful truth: Rules (particularly rules from God and godly parents) are given to provide for and protect you.

Josh and I have learned that when rules are enforced within the context of a loving relationship it generally produces a positive response in our children. In the story, Katie and her parents model this kind of relationship. As our children understand that boundaries are given for their good, our loving relationship with them is reinforced. And ultimately, we want them to come to know that God also says "no" because He wants to protect them and provide for them.

As you instill this basic principle about God and His rules in your child, you'll see it pay off as your child reaches his or her teens. The "WHY WAIT?" campaign is to help prepare teenagers to say no to premarital sex. And we find that those who have understood the motivation behind God's moral restrictions early in life and have a good relationship with their parents are more likely to obey His moral commands in their teen years.

Yours, for helping our youth,

Dottie McDowell

Katie loved her new house. She loved having her very own room. She loved the family room with its cozy fireplace. She loved the big yard to play in. And she especially loved Blueberry Pond down the road. She had never lived near a pond before.

As soon as they moved in, Katie's mom and dad talked
to Katie and her brothers about the pond.

Dad said, "It's great to have a pond near our house.
But nobody is to go to the pond without a grown-up
because it can be dangerous there. We love you very
much and want to protect you."

Katie and her brothers nodded. Katie asked, "Will you
take us to the pond sometimes?"

"Of course." Mom smiled. "We'll have lots of fun over there. Blueberry Pond is one reason we bought this house."

Soon Katie had a new best friend, Sarah. Sarah and Katie did everything together. They walked to the school bus together. They tried to teach their dogs the same tricks. They even had the same favorite colors—pink and purple.

One day Sarah said to Katie, "Let's play at Blueberry Pond. I'll show you where the big old turtle lives and teach you how to skip stones."

"Is your mom going, too?" Katie asked. "I can't go to the pond without a grown-up."

"That's dumb," Sarah told her. "We won't go *in* the water, just near the edge. Are you scared?"

"No . . . but we've got this rule in my family. Kids don't go to the pond without a grown-up."

Sarah looked at Katie. "No one will know if you go. I won't tell on you. Besides, we're big enough to be at the pond by ourselves."

"I promised. I can't go," Katie explained.

"If you don't go, I'll tell the kids at school that you're a scaredy-cat—and I won't be your best friend anymore!"

The girls looked at each other for a *long* time. At last Katie said slowly, "Well, okay . . . I'll go. But don't *ever* tell my mom."

Sarah showed Katie where the turtle
lived. They skipped stones. Soon Katie
could almost make her stone skip at
least two times.

Then they saw a car coming. "Quick! Get into the bushes," Sarah said as she gave Katie a push. "It's your mom's car."

As Katie's mom drove past, she waved at Sarah. Sarah smiled and waved back. "It's safe, you can come out," she called to Katie.

Katie rubbed her arm as she crawled out. "I don't like that. The bushes scratch. And I don't like hiding from Mom, either."

But soon Katie forgot about her mom and the bushes because the turtle came out of its hiding place. They were having so much fun that they forgot to listen and watch for cars.

All of a sudden the girls heard a car stop behind them.

"Katie, come here right now!"

Katie turned and saw her mom beside the car.

"Do you understand that you've disobeyed me?" Mom asked.

Katie nodded, "Yes."

"You broke the family rule by coming to the pond, but you also tried to deceive me by hiding in the bushes. That's like lying."

Katie was quiet as she and her mom drove home. Mom reached over and held Katie's hand for a moment. "When Dad gets home we'll talk about this together."

Katie just nodded.

When Dad came in, Katie hugged him and said, "I'm sorry, Dad, for disobeying you and Mom. I went to Blueberry Pond without a grown-up and lied to Mom by trying to hide. But Sarah said we were big enough, and besides, no one would like me if I was afraid to go to the pond by myself."

"I understand, Katie," he said. "Still, breaking our pond rule is serious."

"But I asked God to forgive me—and you, too. I *promise* I won't go to the pond again. Ever! Even if *no one* likes me."

"We forgive you, Katie," Mom said gently. "But you must understand how serious a wrong you committed. You could have been hurt, and you must learn from this."

"Are you going to punish me?" Katie asked.

"I want you to come with me to the pond," Dad said as he held out his hand.

Katie held her dad's hand as they walked all the way to the pond without saying a word. Katie felt sad because she knew her dad was disappointed with what she had done. They walked to the edge of the pond and sat down on the bank.

"Katie, do you know why Mom and I made a rule forbidding you to come to the pond without a grown-up?" Dad asked.

Katie thought a moment and said, "Because you don't think I'm big enough to go to the pond by myself."

"No," Dad replied. "We made the rule to protect you. We wanted you to enjoy all the fun a pond can bring by protecting you from its dangers."

He looked into Katie's eyes and spoke more seriously than Katie had ever heard him speak before.

"Katie, I love you very much," Dad said softly, "and the rules I make are for your good. When I was about your age I disobeyed my parents and went to a pond by myself. I thought I was big enough, too. One day while I was alone at the pond I slipped on the muddy bank and fell in." He paused and spoke more slowly. "The pond was very deep at the edge and I didn't know how to swim. I thought I was going to drown."

"What happened?" Katie asked.
"How did you get out?"
"When I hit the bottom, I jumped.
As I came to the top, my hand caught
a tree branch that hung over the
water. I pulled myself out knowing that
I could have drowned."

Katie saw Dad's lip quiver and a tear run down his face. Katie began to cry, too.

"Katie," he said, "disobeying is serious. It almost caused me to drown. I don't want that to happen to you."

Katie hugged her dad and said, "I understand now. You made the rule to protect me because you love me."

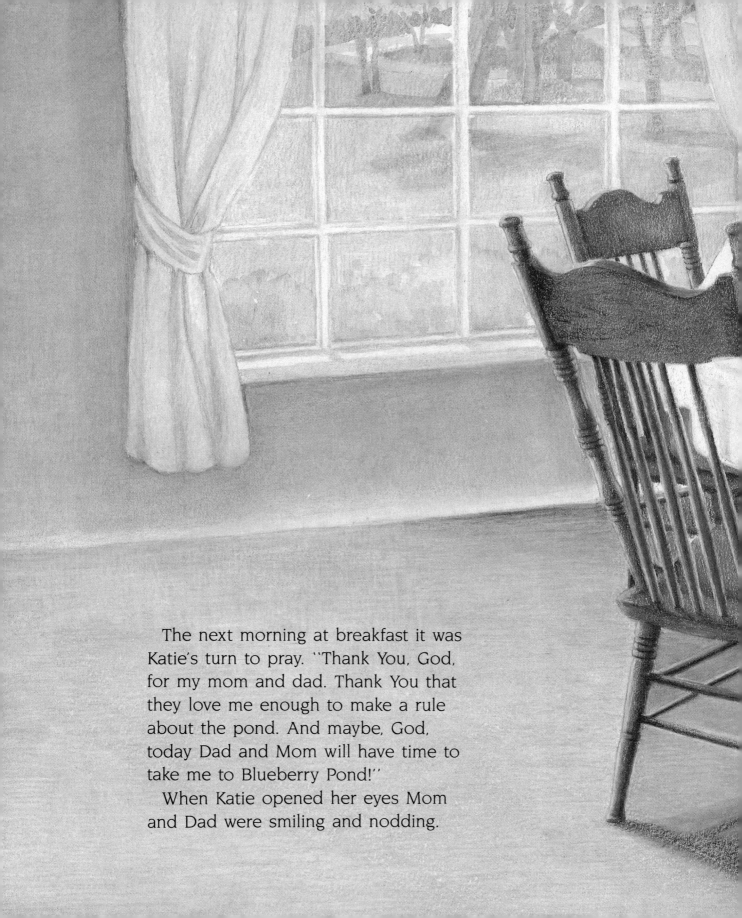

The next morning at breakfast it was Katie's turn to pray. "Thank You, God, for my mom and dad. Thank You that they love me enough to make a rule about the pond. And maybe, God, today Dad and Mom will have time to take me to Blueberry Pond!"

When Katie opened her eyes Mom and Dad were smiling and nodding.

That morning they went to the pond together.